Sigfried's Smelly Socks!

Words and Pictures by:
Len Foley

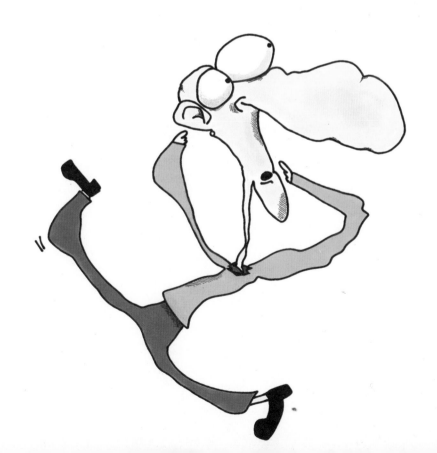

To Becky and Sofia, whose never-ending pile of socks inspired this story.

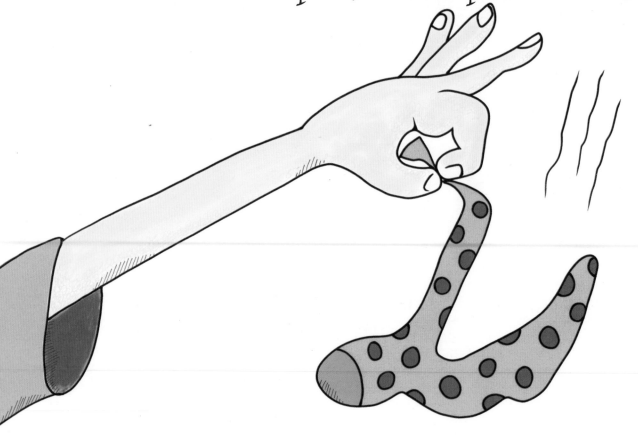

Text © 2017 Len Foley
Pictures © 2017 Len Foley
Cover and internal design © 2017 Len Foley

Special thanks to Katherine Mottram (for her helpful suggestions) and Jennifer Mundy (who was the first person to read it to a room full of kids).

Published by:
New Horizon Health, Inc.
3111 Adirondack Court
Westlake Village, CA 91362

ISBN: 978-0-88692-2

The illustrations in this book were created with the iPad Pro.

Something **stinks** about this book.

Go on and take a **whiff**.

It's a terrible smell as I'm sure you can tell...

But do you have any idea what **it is?**

Perhaps it was the rotten banana that I left on the page

right here

Or maybe the squish-mushed chewing gum I stuck in this book last year?

Could it be
the 'ol pizza slice
that marked my place
as I read?

Or the peanut butter
and jelly chunks
I let dribble off
my bread.

The yellow stain
on this page
is where my naughty dog Oscar

PEED.

And the terrible smell
in this spot
is from something
I can't even **see!**

Hey! What's that terrible smell?

Here is where
I cleaned this page
by spraying it with a

hose...

It's the only place
in this whole silly book
where my brother Sherman
wiped his nose!

And the worst smell yet
is one I regret...
It came from my sister
Piper...

She used this page
to wipe her behind
after she dirtied
her disgusting diaper!

But nothing compares to
the other smell that burns
the hairs on my

head

My orange socks
smell like rotten cabbage...

And my blue socks
smell like skunk feet..

My green socks
smell like ostrich breath...

And my red socks
smell like a toilet seat!

My polka-dot socks smell like dog slobber.

My striped socks smell like kraut.

And I won't let you
near my purple socks...

Because you'd probably
pass out!

It's probably because
of this thing here

Left by my **uncle**
Kato.

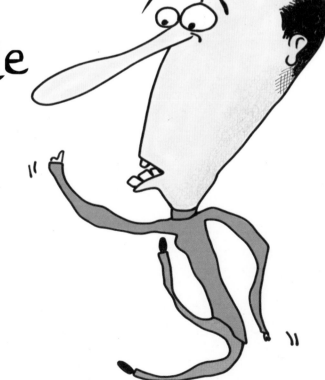

Uncle Kato spilled some ketchup too...

Sow lard and baked beans.

He dribbled turnip clumps and blubber lumps....

And spagetti that's turning green!

I have no idea
what he left right here...

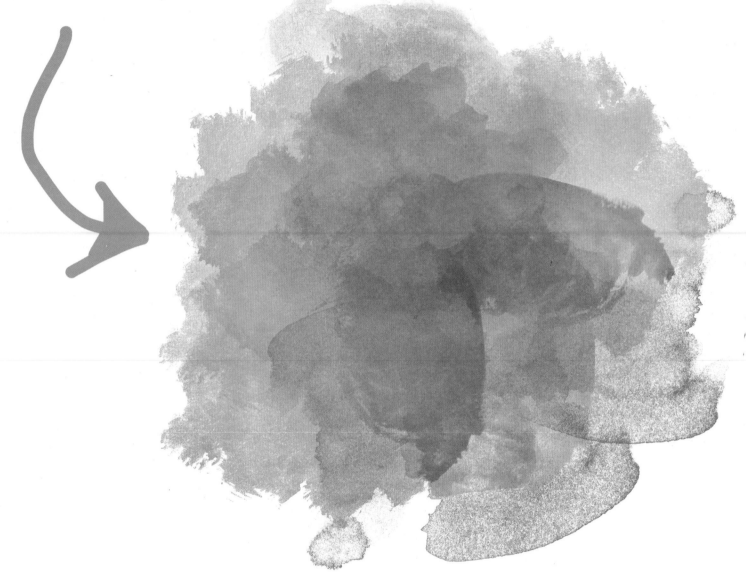

But it reeks of
something awful.

And the yellow splotch
that's on this page...

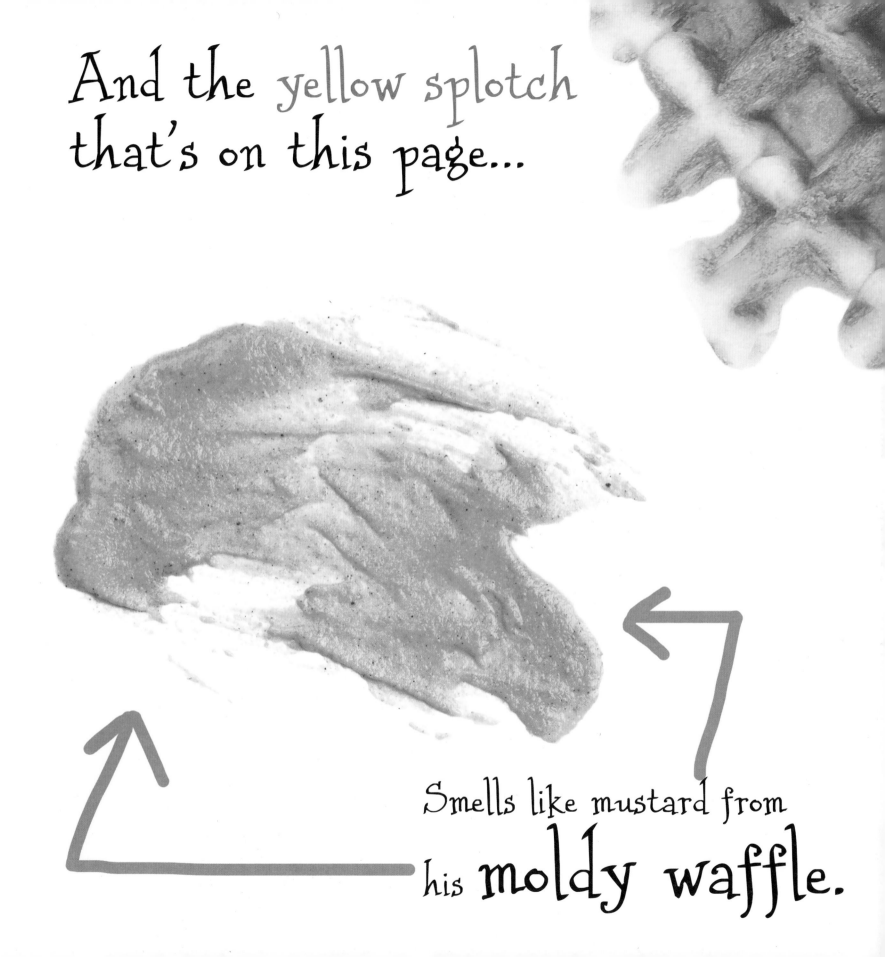

Smells like mustard from
his **moldy waffle.**

Compared to everything else inside this book...

My socks don't cause much trouble.

I **promise** I'll wash my **smelly socks...**